MUSIC MACHINE

By Dusti Bowling

Aven Green

MUSIC MACHINE

DUSTI BOWLING
illustrated by GINA PERRY

union
square
kids

NEW YORK

**union
square
kids**

NEW YORK

ISBN 978-1-4549-4222-1 (hardcover)
ISBN 978-1-4549-4186-6 (e-book)

Library of Congress Cataloging-in-Publication Data

Names: Bowling, Dusti, author. | Perry, Gina, illustrator.
Title: Aven Green music machine / Dusti Bowling ; illustrated by Gina Perry.
Description: New York : Union Square Kids, [2022] | Series: Aven Green | Audience: Ages 6 to 8. | Audience: Grades 2-3. | Summary: Eight-year-old Aven Green is despondent when she does not master the piano in one day, but with new inspiration from guitarist Mr. Tom, who is armless like her, along with a special gift from her great-grandma, Aven learns she does not need to be perfect to perform.
Identifiers: LCCN 2022009872 (print) | LCCN 2022009873 (ebook) | ISBN 9781454942221 (hardback) | ISBN 9781454941866 (ebook)
Subjects: CYAC: People with disabilities--Fiction. | Musicians--Fiction. Talent shows--Fiction. | Schools--Fiction. | Self-acceptance--Fiction. | Fiction. lcgft | BISAC: JUVENILE FICTION / Disabilities & Special Needs | JUVENILE FICTION / Family / Adoption
Classification: LCC PZ7.1.B6872 Av 2022 (print) | LCC PZ7.1.B6872 (ebook) | DDC [Fic]--dc23
LC record available at https://lccn.loc.gov/2022009872
LC ebook record available at https://lccn.loc.gov/2022009873

For information about custom editions, special sales, and premium purchases, please contact specialsales@unionsquareandco.com.

Printed in Canada
Lot #:
2 4 6 8 10 9 7 5 3 1
06/22

unionsquareandco.com

Cover illustration by Marta Kissi

For my Book Hooks

Contents

Chapter 1

Professional Musician Requirements

There are a lot of important musical events in elementary school—choir performances, plays, talent shows, and singing "Raining Tacos" at the top of your lungs on the bus with your friends until the bus driver, Mr. Munck, threatens to throw you all out the window. Don't worry, he's just joking with us and has never actually done that. Or else he'd probably be fired.

I want to be a big part of all these important musical events, and that's why I've decided I am going to learn to play an instrument. *Professionally.* Professionally means you get paid for what you do. How am I going to get paid while I'm still a kid? Well, when people hear me play my beautiful music, they won't be able to stop themselves from throwing money into my fishbowl. I've seen that happen in the mall lobby with the piano player guy.

But I won't play the instrument just like anyone else. I'll have to play it with my feet because, you see, I don't have arms. Yep, you heard me. No arms here on my torso, which I'd like to add is already eight years old.

That means if I play the flute, I'll have to hold it with my feet. And if I play the piano, I'll have to hit the keys with my toes. And if I decide to play the accordion, the most beautiful instrument of all time, I'll have to play it with my belly button. Just kidding, of course. That would be silly. My belly button isn't nearly as talented as my feet.

There are several requirements for becoming a professional musician. The first requirement is having fabulous taste in music. I listen to all kinds of music—rock, pop, country, and polka (because lots of accordion, of course!). I've even listened to *Mozart*. Mom made me because she said it was good for my brain. I'm pretty sure she's right, because my brain grew even more brain cells after I listened to it.

Another requirement is having a really good memory. I can remember all the *lyrics* to "The Song that Never Ends" and "Raining Tacos." Lyrics are just the words in a song, in case you were wondering.

Another requirement is having a super-powered brain full of extra brain cells like mine. You couldn't even hear music or sing music or play music without a brain, so this might be the most important requirement of all.

But you know what's not a requirement for becoming a professional musician? Having arms, that's what.

Chapter 2

So Many Talents

Ms. Luna wrote something on the board while Emily whispered to me that she should come to my house after school one day this week. I thought that was Emily's best idea in a long time.

When Ms. Luna stepped away, we could see that she wrote the words TALENT SHOW on the board, and we all got really excited. "I'm so happy to tell you we're going to have a talent show next week," she said.

"But what if we don't have a talent?" asked Ren.

"You have lots of talents," I told him. "You build beautiful birds from LEGOs and make delicious steamed bean cakes."

Ren smiled at me. "Thanks, Aven," he said, his cheeks all pink.

"Aven's right," said Ms. Luna. "Everyone has a talent. Maybe it's drawing or singing or baking cakes or building LEGO birds." She winked at Ren, and he got even pinker. "We can all do something special." She looked around at all of us like she was sizing up our talents with her big brown eyes. "So, what do you like to do?"

Robert's hand shot up, and Ms. Luna called on him. "I like to play video games," he said.

Ms. Luna nodded. "Okay. Being good at video games can certainly be a talent, but I'm not sure how you'd show it to people at the talent show."

Robert scratched his head. "I can also sniff a whole spaghetti noodle up my nose," he said. "And pull it out of my mouth."

"*Ew*," said Kayla. "I sure hope you cook it first because I think that would hurt."

Ms. Luna covered her mouth and looked like she was feeling a little bit sick for a second before saying, "I guess you can show people that if you really want to at the talent show."

"I do," said Robert. "I really do."

A girl named Stacy, who was on my soccer team, raised her hand and stood up. "I'm really good at cheerleading," she said. Then she jumped and did some wild kicks in the air and screamed out, "Go Sticker Kickers!"

Emily, Kayla, and I all clapped, because that was the name of our soccer team.

"Very nice, Stacy," said Ms. Luna. Then she turned her head to Emily, who had her hand raised. "Yes, Emily?"

Emily stood up and smoothed down her purple jumper. "I am the best at painting fingernails," she said, waving her purple fingernails at all of us and waggling her unibrow.

Ms. Luna grinned and said, "That's wonderful. And sparkly too."

"I *only* have sparkly nail polish," said Emily. "Because that's the best kind. And also I am good at poems."

"You write poems?" Ms. Luna asked.

Emily got a far-off look on her face as she stared at the cat poster in the corner. She said, "Behold, the cat, hanging from the tree. Will he fall and splat on the ground? Or will he fly over the clouds and go all the way up into freezing space where he can't breathe because there's no air up there? Good thing he has nine lives."

The class all snickered, but Ms. Luna said, "That was . . . beautiful. Maybe you can write a poem for the talent show."

Emily curtsied and sat down as Ms. Luna turned to me. "How about you, Aven?" she asked. "I know you have many talents."

I collapsed tiredly down in my seat. "Where do I even begin?" I said, then I sat up straighter and took a deep breath. "I am the best at solving mysteries. I am an expert baker. I am almost ready to play soccer at the Olympics. And I am a professional musician."

Ms. Luna's eyes lit up. "Oh, do you play an instrument? I didn't know that."

"Yes, I do," I said. "I'm just not sure which one."

Ms. Luna nodded, though she looked a little confused. "So you haven't picked an instrument yet?"

"How could I?" I declared. "There are so many—the horn, the saxophone, the accordion, the kazoo! How can I ever decide? I want to play them all."

Ms. Luna smiled. "I suggest trying them out one by one," she said. "Get a good feel for each one to see which instrument you enjoy the most."

Ms. Luna was really onto something there. I'd be sure to share this excellent plan with Mom the moment I got home from school.

Kayla raised her hand, and Ms. Luna called on her. Kayla stood up and looked down her nose at the rest of us. "Well," she said. "Since I won the baking contest at the county fair last week, it's clear that I have the best baking talent of everyone in all of Kansas City."

I did my best not to roll my eyes at her because rolling your eyes at your friends is not nice. Neither is glaring your eyes at them. Or giving them the stink eye. "Emily and Sujata won, too!" I called out instead, not even adding that they only won third place. "So you have a three-way tie for best baker." I looked at Sujata, and she gave me a huge smile.

Kayla cleared her throat. "Anyway, before I was so rudely interrupted," she said. "I could bring in a delicious dessert for the talent show."

"That's a good idea, Kayla," said Ms. Luna. "I'm sure we'd all love to sample it."

"I can also do ballet," said Kayla, running around the room and doing some very lovely jumping and spinning and kicking that I recognized from our ninja competitions. I didn't know ballet helped so much with ninja competitions.

"Wow," said Ms. Luna. "That is wonderful, Kayla. We'd love to see more of your ballet at the talent show."

Ren asked Ms. Luna what her talents were, and then we all wanted to know. "Yeah, Ms. Luna!" I cried. "Tell us about your talent. What are you good at?"

Ms. Luna blushed. "The talent show is just for students. And I really don't have any talents."

"But you said everyone can do something special," I said, then sighed. "I guess you lied."

Ms. Luna's eyes grew big. "Okay, you got me, Aven," she said, laughing. "I do have a special talent."

"What is it?" asked Ren.

"My boyfriend and I enjoy dancing," she said. "And I think we're quite good at *zapateado*, which is like tap dancing."

We all stared at her quietly, the only sound in the room the ticking clock and a few sniffles. I knew everyone was shocked. Shocked, I tell you! Finally, Emily said, "You have a *boyfriend*?"

Ms. Luna looked around the room at all the staring faces, then laughed. "Yes, I do. Have I never mentioned him before to you?"

We all shook our heads.

"Is he a teacher?" asked Kayla.

"Nope," said Ms. Luna. "He's a firefighter."

"Has he ever put out a fire?" asked Ren.

"Oh yes," said Ms. Luna. "Lots of times."

The whole class made *oh* and *ah* sounds to show how impressed we were.

"Is he an old man?" asked Robert.

Ms. Luna laughed again. "He's my age," she said.

Robert nodded. "So he's a *super* old man."

Ms. Luna stopped laughing, and she cleared her throat. "Anyway, the talent show isn't for me. It's for you, and I can't wait to see all your amazing talents."

I sat in my seat, grinning. Yep, just wait until they saw my amazing musical talent. I sure hoped they were all wearing extra socks because I was going to knock their first pair right off.

Chapter 3

The Music Store

That day after school, Mom and I talked about which instrument I should start learning for the talent show. I instantly suggested the accordion because nothing makes more beautiful sounds and melodies than the accordion.

"Well," said Mom. "I just don't know if the accordion is the best choice right now, Aven. Why don't you start with an instrument that you can handle well with your feet?"

"Don't you mean an instrument that I can *feetle* well with my feet?" I said.

She nodded. "Yes, that's exactly what I meant. I was thinking possibly piano because we could get a keyboard to place at your feet."

I imagined sitting up in front of my class, playing Mozart on a keyboard with my feet, and I liked that thought very much. I wondered how long it would take me to learn a Mozart song. The talent show was the next week, and it shouldn't even take that long. "Oh, I think that's a good idea," I said.

She clapped her hands together. "Wonderful," she said. "We can start with a keyboard. That way you can sit in a chair or on the couch while you play. You could even sit on the floor if that works best. Really, you can play it anyway and anywhere you feel most comfortable."

"Okay," I said excitedly.

"How about we go to the music store to see what kind of keyboards we might be able to rent?" she said.

"Rent?" I asked, remembering the bounce house Mom and Dad rented for my birthday party. They only let us have it for four hours! I could probably learn Mozart in four hours if I needed to, but I might want to learn Beethoven, too. "I want to buy one," I said.

"If we rent," Mom explained, "we can return it if you don't enjoy it. And then we can rent another instrument to try. Once you find one you love, then we can buy it."

"Can we keep it longer than four hours?" I asked.

She smiled. "Of course! I'm sure they rent them by the month."

Wow. In a whole month I could probably learn Mozart, Beethoven, and even "Raining Tacos." I wondered if I could drag a keyboard onto the bus.

Mom and I got into the car, and Mom put on our favorite music station while I did toe stretches in my seat. "What are you doing with your feet?" asked Mom.

"Stretching my toes," I said. "So I can reach even more keys."

"Your toes will also keep getting longer," said Mom. "So that will help."

We pulled up to the music store and went inside, where a man met us at the door. "Well, hello, ladies," he said cheerfully. "What can I help you with today?"

Mom put her arm around my shoulders. "My daughter would like to try out a keyboard. Do you have any for rent?"

The man looked down at me and glanced at my shoulders for a moment. I was pretty sure he was wondering if I was hiding my arms for some reason, but if he asked me about it, I would definitely not say, "Yeah, I'm hiding them up your nose!" which is what I said to a kid at school one time and had to stay in from recess that day. Missing recess was the worst.

"How wonderful," the man finally said. "Let's go check out some of our rentals to see which one might work best for her."

Chapter 4

The "Welcome Home, Dad" Song

The man at the music store actually ended up being pretty nice, and he didn't act funny about me using my feet on the keyboards. He also recommended a piano teacher for us to try.

I couldn't wait to show Dad the new keyboard when he got home from work that night. Mom helped me set it up in the living room so that when he walked in, he could hear me pounding on the keys to greet him. I called it my "Welcome Home, Dad" song.

"Listen to that!" he declared, clapping his hands and smiling big when he walked in. "Do I hear a musician in the house?"

"You do!" I cried, still pounding on the keys. "And it's me! It's me, Dad! I'm the musician!"

"I can see *and* hear that," he said, sitting down next to me on the couch and bobbing his head to my amazing piano playing.

"And she has a lesson already after school tomorrow," said Mom. "With a Ms. Fernsby."

"Ms. Fernsby," Dad repeated. "Sounds like a good teacher."

"I sure hope she knows Mozart," I said. "Because that's what I want to learn tomorrow."

"Wow," said Dad. "That's a great big goal, Aven. Maybe that's a good *long-term* goal. Not a goal for tomorrow?"

I snorted and rolled my eyes. "Dad," I said. "Of course, I have lots of long-term goals. Like becoming the greatest piano player who ever lived."

"A piano player is called a *pianist*," Dad said.

"I'm going to be the world's great pianist then," I said.

Dad nodded. "Well, whatever you learn tomorrow will be great. You just have to do your best."

"And my best is magnificent," I declared.

Dad put an arm around me while I continued playing "Welcome Home, Dad."

"I think it is, too," he said.

Chapter 5

Too Many Musical Notes

Mom drove us to Ms. Fernsby's house the next day after school. An old lady with a gray bun and glasses answered the door and shook Mom's hand. "I'm so happy to meet you," the lady said.

"Nice to meet you, Ms. Fernsby," said Mom. Then she patted my head. "This is Aven."

Ms. Fernsby nodded. "Hello, Aven. Come in, please."

Ms. Fernsby led us to this big, beautiful piano in the middle of her living room. We sat down

side-by-side on the piano bench and Mom sat in a puffy chair nearby. "So how much training does Aven have?" Ms. Fernsby asked.

"None at all," said Mom.

"But I do have natural musical talent," I told Ms. Fernsby.

Ms. Fernsby laughed. "I'm sure you do," she said. "I have to admit, I've never had a student like you before."

"A student with natural musical talent?" I asked.

Ms. Fernsby laughed again, though I wasn't sure why. "Go ahead and slip your shoes off, Aven," she told me, and I pushed my blue polka-dotted flats off.

Ms. Fernsby pointed at a key in the middle of the piano. "Aven, this is middle C. Can you play that with your toes?"

I lifted my foot and tapped middle C with my big toe.

"Very good," said Ms. Fernsby, but I was already losing my balance, and I sort of fell over off the piano bench in slow motion.

"Oh no!" Ms. Fernsby declared as I face-planted into the carpet.

Mom stood from her puffy chair. "You okay, Aven?" she asked. I was okay, except for my mouthful of carpet hairs. I hoped Ms. Fernsby vacuumed regularly.

Mom helped me back onto the bench, telling Ms. Fernsby, "Aven's been practicing on a keyboard at home. She sits on the couch with the keyboard at her feet."

Ms. Fersnby nodded. "I can see why this would be challenging then," she said. "Normally at a first lesson, we would learn about fingering and posture, but of course all of that will be different for Aven."

I managed to keep my balance after that while Mrs. Fernsby showed me all the C notes. Then we decided what we would call my toes. "I would like to call my big toe Francesca," I said. "And my pinky toe should be Becky."

Mrs. Fernsby laughed again. She sure did a lot of laughing. "Aven, I think we should number them like we number fingers." So she called my big toe, Toe One, and my pinky toe, Toe Five. You can probably guess what we called the others. What boring names for my toes!

Then, guess what? The lesson was already over. "But I haven't even learned Mozart yet," I said.

"Learning the piano takes time, Aven," said Mrs. Fernsby. "You can't learn Mozart at your first lesson. You have to learn all the *musical notes* first."

"How many musical notes are there?" I asked.

Mrs. Fernsby cleared her throat and opened a book that was sitting on the piano. She pointed at the notes in the music. "Well, there's A, B, C, D, E, F, and G for the white keys."

"But that's too many notes!" I declared. "I only learned C today and there are six more notes. That will take too long to learn. I need to know Mozart by the talent show."

Mom stood up and grabbed her purse. "Aven, whatever you've learned by then will be great for the talent show. No one expects you to learn Mozart in a single lesson."

We said goodbye to Mrs. Fernsby, and I sulked in my seat all the way home. If I was only going to learn one note a week, that meant I would only be able to play two notes by the talent show. I could picture myself up on stage, just hitting two stupid keys with Toe One. Who'd want to watch that? Nobody, that's who.

Chapter 6

So Much Spying

At lunch the next day at school, everyone was blabbing on and on about their talents. It turned out this kid in my class named Stephen could balance a spoon on his nose for ten whole seconds. And another kid named Devon could stand on one leg for over a minute. And another kid named Suzy could make farting noises with her armpits. All their impressive talents just made me feel worse.

"So, what are you going to do, Aven?" Kayla asked after showing us more of her ballet moves.

"I'm going to play the piano," I said.

"What song are you going to play?" asked Sujata.

"I'm going to play note C," I said. "And possibly one other note."

Everyone around the lunch table just stared at me. "That's it?" said Kayla. "That's all you're going to play?"

I forced out a laugh even though I felt

terrible inside. I *knew* no one would want to watch me play two notes. "Of course not!" I said. "Of course, that's not all. I'm also going to play a really good song, but it's going to be a surprise."

I'd just have to teach myself some songs if Ms. Fernsby wasn't going to teach me. I'd taught myself all kinds of things—how to put on my underwear and brush my teeth and hair and even make an ice cream sundae. All without help. I could learn to play the piano without help, too.

Emily leaned over and whispered, "But you'll show me after school right?"

I got this sick, rumbly feeling in my stomach, but I nodded. "Yes, of course I'll show you," I told her.

"Great!" said Emily. "And I'll read you some of my poems I've written."

I gulped. I didn't even feel like finishing my peanut butter and jelly sandwich anymore. When we got back to class, Ms. Luna let us have quiet reading time. Sujata, Ren, and I took the beanbags in the corner, but Sujata and Ren kept whispering about their talents to each other, so I had a really hard time focusing on my reading because I was secretly spying on their conversation.

"What's your talent?" whispered Ren to Sujata.

Sujata put her book down and whispered,

"I'm going to sing a song."

"I didn't know you could sing," whispered Ren.

I looked up from my book, which I held open on the floor with my toes. "Me neither!" I declared.

Ms. Luna had been walking around the room, peeking at everyone's book choices, but she stopped and looked at me from across the room. "Aven, it's *quiet* reading time," she said.

I pretended to go back to my book, but when Ms. Luna wasn't looking at me anymore, I whispered to Sujata, "What song are you going to sing?"

Sujata whispered, "Somewhere Over the Rainbow."

"I bet your voice is beautiful," whispered Ren.

Sujata blushed and went back to her book, but I whispered to Ren, "What about my

piano playing? Don't you bet my piano playing will be beautiful?"

Ren nodded quickly. "I'm sure you'll play
note C very beautifully," he said.

"I told you I'm going to play a whole song,"
I whispered.

Ms. Luna said, "Aven, please go sit somewhere else."

My cheeks got all hot as I closed my book
and slipped it between my chin and shoulder.

Then I walked across the room without looking at anyone and flopped down next to Kayla and Emily. But they were also whispering about their talents, which meant now I had to spy on them.

"Just wait until you see my ballet dance," whispered Kayla. "It will be the best one I've ever done."

"And my poem will make everyone cry," whispered Emily. "But in a good way."

I didn't get any reading done that day because I just kept feeling worse and worse. I wasn't sure I was going to knock anyone's socks off anymore. They'd probably stay right on their feet.

Chapter 7

Bad Noises

When we got to my house after school that day, Mom made us a snack of apple slices with peanut butter. I was glad, too. I hadn't been able to finish my lunch because I'd felt all sick. Then Emily read me her newest poem, which she called "Apple Slices with Peanut Butter."

I was pretty sure she just made it up while we were eating.

"Now show me what you're going to do on the piano," said Emily.

I gulped and led her to the keyboard in the living room. Then I sat down on the couch and turned the power on with my toes. "This is middle C," I told her, tapping it with my toe. "And these are the rest of the C notes." I tapped them all from left to right.

"But what else can you do?" asked Emily. "I want to hear the song you're going to play."

"Right," I said, taking a big breath, my heart pounding. "This is a special song I wrote for my dad. I hope you like it." Then I played my "Welcome Home, Dad" song for her.

Emily got a funny look on her face.

She pressed her hands over her ears. Then she squinted her eyes shut and started shaking her head.

I stopped playing. "What's wrong?" I asked.

"That's the worst song I ever heard in my life," she said.

My whole heart sank all the way down into Toes One, Two, Three, Four, and Five. "That was the meanest thing anyone has ever said to me," I said.

"Well, it's true," she said. "It didn't even have a *melody*."

I stared down at my keyboard. "Yes, it did."

"No, it didn't," said Emily. "I know what a melody sounds like. It's when a bunch of notes sound good when they're put together. Your notes all sounded bad together."

"Dad likes it," I said softly.

Emily rolled her eyes. "Of course he does. He's your dad. He has to like your bad noises."

Bad noises. Like my piano playing sounded like a big loud stinky toot or something.

"Just watch this," said Emily, and she stretched her fingers out and played note C and also two other keys at the same time. "That's a whole *chord*. My brother taught me that." She looked up at me. "Can you play a whole chord, Aven?"

I tried, but no matter how much I stretched my toes, I couldn't reach all three keys at the same time like Emily had. And I kept hitting other keys instead. So it just sounded like more bad noises.

Emily shook her head and said, "Maybe you should do something else for the talent show."

I felt like crying. "But I already told everyone I was going to play a song on the piano."

Emily shrugged. "It's okay to change your mind. And you really wouldn't want to force your bad noises on anyone."

I really wished she would stop saying the words *bad noises*. I didn't feel like doing anything else with Emily after that. I didn't even want to play stuffy salon or have a ninja competition or paint our nails or anything. My feelings were too hurt.

Chapter 8

Made for Toes?

Finally, Emily's mom picked her up to take her home, and Mom, Dad, and I sat down for dinner. Mom had made one of my favorites, pantry surprise, but not even pantry surprise could cheer me up.

"What's the matter, Sheebs?" Dad asked.

I frowned at my pantry surprise, which looked like a mix of spaghetti noodles, tuna, and broccoli cheese soup. Pantry surprise was always different. That was the surprise. "Emily thinks I'm a terrible piano player," I said.

"Well, honey, you've only had one lesson," said Mom.

"But Emily could play three keys at once. I can't stretch my toes enough to even do that. And she said 'Welcome Home, Dad' sounded like bad noises."

"I love that song," Dad said. "And also that's a matter of opinion. Everyone's musical taste is different. One person's 'bad noises' may be another person's favorite song. I remember when I was young, and I would listen to my favorite band: Barfing Baby Dolls. My mom said it sounded like bad noises. But I thought it sounded awesome."

Mom was looking at Dad with her mouth wide open. "You listened to a band called Barfing Baby Dolls?" she asked.

"Oh yeah," said Dad. "I think I still have a CD around somewhere. I can play some of their music for you sometime."

"No, thank you," Mom said quickly.

"I don't think I can learn the piano anymore," I said. "I even fell off the bench at Ms. Fernsby's. I still have carpet in between my teeth."

"Honey," Mom said, patting me on the back. "You've barely even begun. You should give it a real chance."

My eyes filled with tears. "I don't want to give it a chance," I said. "Piano keys were made for fingers. Not toes."

"Nonsense," said Dad. He held up his fork. "Was this fork made for toes? Probably not. But you still do a good job with it."

I stared at my forkful of pantry surprise held in between my toes. "It's not like holding a fork, Dad. It's way harder than that."

Dad got up and walked to the junk drawer. He pulled out a pencil and said, "Was this pencil made for toes?"

I shook my head and said, "No, it was not."

Then Dad pulled out a pair of scissors. "And these scissors," he said. "Were they made for toes?"

"Those are the danger scissors, Dad!" I cried. "Those things almost cut off Toe Five!"

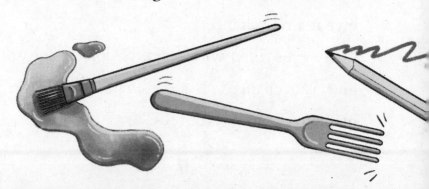

Dad grimaced and threw them back in the junk drawer. Then he said, "*Aha!*" and pulled out a paintbrush. "You have made many beautiful paintings with this paintbrush. Was *it* made for toes?"

I shook my head. "What exactly are you getting at?" I asked.

Dad sighed and sat back down at the table. "Aven, I'm just trying to show you that even though something isn't made for your toes, that doesn't mean you can't use it. The same thing goes for instruments."

"But it's too hard," I said. "My toes can't stretch enough. It's impossible."

"Don't forget your feet are going to grow

and get bigger," Mom said. "You'll be able to stretch and reach farther all the time."

"It will take me a hundred years to grow feet big enough to play Mozart," I said. "No matter how hard I try, I just can't stretch far enough to play notes like Emily."

"Well, Aven," Mom said, "we did agree you could try out different instruments. So if you feel the piano's not right for you, then you can try something else. I want you to enjoy your instrument. Playing music should make you happy, and you look very unhappy right now."

"I am, Mom," I declared. "I'm very unhappy."

"Okay then," said Mom. "Tomorrow we'll go back to the music store and try something else."

Chapter 9

The Only Disappointing Thing

The nice man at the music store was very understanding about us wanting to return the keyboard and try a different instrument. But when I tried to hold the recorder with my feet, it slipped out of my grip. And the drumsticks kept flying out of my toes when I tried the drums. One almost hit the nice man in the eye! And don't even ask about the tuba and violin. Disasters, people. Disasters.

"I guess we'll just have to keep trying," Mom said on the way home from the music store.

I sniffled and looked out the car window. "I don't want to try any more instruments," I said. "I'm not the musician I thought I was."

"Aven," Mom said, sighing. "You haven't given it a good enough chance. It's only been a few days since you decided to learn an instrument."

"I've tried every instrument on earth, Mom," I said, wiping my cheek on my shoulder.

"Not every instrument," said Mom.

"I think I'll just stay home from school that day," I said. "I don't even want to go to the talent show."

Mom shook her head and said, "The Aven I know doesn't hide from a challenge. She meets it head on."

"Well, my head's just not on for this one," I declared. "My head is definitely off."

"That's . . . not what I meant, Aven," Mom said. "What I meant was that you usually go after a challenge and do the best you can. All you can do is your best, and that's good enough always. I could never be disappointed in you for doing your best."

"But this time my best is just bad noises," I said. "Big bad disappointing noises."

Mom clucked her tongue. "You, Aven Green, are giving up too fast. And that's the only disappointing thing about all of this."

Chapter 10

All You Can Do

"So has everyone decided on what they're doing for the talent show?" Ms. Luna asked at school the next day.

Robert stood up. "Definitely the spaghetti noodle trick," he said.

Ms. Luna frowned. "I'm sure we'll all enjoy that, Robert." Then she looked at me. "How about you, Aven? Did you find an instrument you like yet?"

I sighed. "Ms. Luna, I am not the expert musician I thought I was. I've tried the piano,

the drums, the recorder, the tuba, and the
violin. I stink, and I don't care who knows it."
I glanced around the room. Yep. Everyone
knew it.

Ms. Luna gave me a warm smile. "I'm sure
that's not true, Aven. You only just told me

you were going to learn an instrument a few days ago. No one can learn to play like an expert that quickly."

"Well, I don't have enough time to learn anything for the talent show," I said, hunching down in my seat.

"Aven," said Ms. Luna. "Do you think the expert musicians you see learned to play like that in a week? Of course not. They've had years of practice. Please don't give up so quickly." She looked around the room. "That goes for all of you. Most talents take lots of practice. People don't become experts overnight."

"I got the spaghetti noodle trick right on my first try," said Robert, smirking. "No practice necessary."

Ms. Luna sighed. "That's really impressive, Robert." she said. "But the rest of us need lots of time to grow our talents. I certainly didn't learn how to dance zapateado overnight. It took lots of practice. But I'm glad I didn't give up when I couldn't do it perfectly right away. And I enjoyed the learning process as well."

Ms. Luna walked over to my desk. "Aven," she said. "You'll never know what your real talents are if you give up quickly when things are hard."

"But what's the point of doing something if I'm not an expert at it?" I asked her. "People will just laugh at me."

"If you're learning something and growing and doing your best and getting better at it all the time, then what's there to laugh at?" asked Ms. Luna.

I gave Emily the stink eye and said, "Bad noises."

Ms. Luna put a hand on my shoulder. "One day those noises will turn into beautiful

noises, but you can't ever get there if you give up." Then Ms. Luna looked around the room. "And no one, and I mean *no one*, will be laughing at anyone's talents. Got it?"

We all nodded in agreement. Then Kayla raised her hand. "But we can laugh at Robert's, right?" she asked. "Or gag? Can we at least gag? We might not be able to help it."

Ms. Luna took in deep breath and said, "We'll just have to do our best to give everyone the respect they deserve. All we can do is our best." She looked down at me. "That goes for you, too, Aven. You can't do better than your best. As long as you do your best, you can feel good about that."

Chapter 11

What a Coincidence

The next day was Saturday, so I decided to do some good soul-searching at home. That's what Great-grandma called it when you thought really hard about something.

I'd only done one lesson with the piano. And I *had* liked playing the keyboard on the floor until Emily hurt my feelings. And I'd hardly given any of the other instruments a good shot.

I finally left my room after *ten* full minutes of soul-searching and found Mom and

Dad sitting at the kitchen table drinking coffee.

"And how's my Sheebs this morning?" Dad asked.

"I think I've almost found my soul," I said. "But I might need to do a little more searching."

Dad smiled and asked, "Could you do the rest of your soul-searching on a little road trip?"

"Where are we going?" I asked.

"St. Louis," said Dad. "But we have a long drive. Four whole hours, so we better get moving."

"Four hours?" I asked. "Why are we going all the way there?"

"It's a special surprise," said Dad.

Because our drive was so long, I made sure to bring lots of books to read and toys to play with in the car, but I still got bored because four hours is even longer than forever. I was so bored I even fell asleep!

We finally got to St. Louis around lunchtime, and we stopped and got barbecue sandwiches before Dad drove us to a coffee shop.

"We drove four hours to go to a *coffee* place?" I asked. "I know you guys like coffee, but I also think maybe you've gone a little bit bananas."

Dad laughed. "They have something even better than good coffee," he said.

We all walked in, and Mom and Dad ordered coffee, and I got a hot chocolate.

Then we sat down at a little table in front of a small open area that had some speakers and a chair and a guitar on the floor. I shook my head and said, "I still can't believe you guys drove us all the way to St. Louis to go to a coffee place. Grown-ups are so weird."

Mom and Dad looked at each other and smiled. Then we sipped our drinks quietly until this guy walked out to the little stage area. And guess what? He didn't have arms—like me!

The man noticed me, and his face lit up. "Hey there, little lady," he said.

"Hello, fellow armless person," I said.

The guy laughed. "My name's Luke," he said. "What's yours?"

"Aven," I said. "I'm from Kansas City, and I'm eight years old."

He laughed again. "I'm from St. Louis and I'm forty-five years old." Then he sat down in the chair and moved the guitar in front of him with his feet, strumming it a few times and turning the little knobs. "I hope you enjoy the show, Aven," he said.

I looked at Mom and Dad and whispered, "Can you believe we came all this way for coffee, and there's a guy here without arms who plays the guitar?"

Mom and Dad looked at each other and smiled. "What a coincidence," said Dad.

Chapter 12

Busted

We watched Luke play all kinds of songs—mostly stuff that Mom and Dad like and nothing as good as "Raining Tacos." But, boy, he could play that guitar with his feet better than anyone with hands ever could. I watched his feet the whole time, amazed at how he could move them and stretch them and pluck all those strings with them.

When Luke took a break from playing, he came and sat down at our little table. "Tell

me, Aven," he said. "Do you like to play any
instruments?"

I shrugged, and my good mood fell. "I tried
some," I said. "But I'm not very good."

"Which ones did you try?" asked Luke.

"I tried the piano," I said. "I had one lesson, and I fell off the bench."

He nodded. "One lesson, huh?"

"How long did it take you to learn the guitar, Luke?" asked Mom.

"Let's see," Luke said, looking up at the ceiling like he was thinking hard. "I began playing around Aven's age here, but I'd say I really started catching onto it by about eleven. So three years."

"And how long have you been playing now?" asked Dad.

If Luke started when he was eight and he was forty-five now that meant he'd been playing . . . "Thirty-seven years!" I declared.

Luke laughed. "Someone's good at math," he said.

"That sure is a lot longer than one lesson," said Mom. "Do you have any tips for our Aven?"

Luke gave me a serious look. "Learning an instrument takes lots of practice and patience," he said. "It can be a slow process, and it can be tempting to give up when you don't learn

as fast as you want. But if you stick with it, the rewards are wonderful. I love being able to play the guitar. It brings me so much joy. Have you tried the guitar yet, Aven?"

I shook my head. "No, not yet."

Luke walked over to his music case and removed a card with his toes then handed it to Mom and Dad. "This is a great music store here in St. Louis," he said. "I know the owner. He can help you find the right guitar that will fit your feet if you decide you'd like to try one." Then he grinned. "Hey, how'd you like to try one right now?"

"At the music store?" I asked.

"No," said Luke, sitting down in front of his guitar. "Let's try this guitar right here. Pull up a chair."

Dad moved a chair next to Luke, and I sat down. Then Luke showed me how he pressed a string against something he called a *fret* with his right toe and strummed the strings with his other toes. Then I did the same thing. And guess what? It sounded pretty good!

Mom and Dad clapped. "That's a lovely sound," said Mom.

"Doesn't sound like bad noises at all," said Dad.

"My piano teacher told me about notes A, B, C, D, E, F, and G," I said.

"The guitar has those same notes too," said Luke. Then he plucked a string with is toe. "That's the E string," he explained.

I plucked the E string. "I already learned the E string!" I called to my parents.

They smiled and clapped at their little table. Then Luke showed me a couple more of his good music moves, and we watched him play the rest of his songs. When he was done, we waved goodbye, and Luke said to me, "I'd say you have some natural music talent, Aven. I hope you'll keep playing."

Then we left the coffee shop to head over to the music store Luke told us about. In the car on the way there, I narrowed my eyes at my parents and said, "I think you guys *knew* Luke was going to be there today."

Mom and Dad looked at each other and smiled. "I guess we've been busted," said Mom.

Chapter 13

One Little Riff

Mom took me to visit Great-grandma the next day so I could show her my new guitar and tell her all about St. Louis and meeting Luke and the barbecue sandwiches and the hot chocolate. When we walked in, we found Great-grandma sitting on the couch with Smitty. Great-grandma had on the funniest looking necklace I'd ever seen in my whole entire life! It stuck way up in front of her face.

"Hi, honey," she said, a great big smile on her old mouth, which I could barely see

because the funny necklace was covering it.

"What's that weird thing you've got on, Grandma?" I asked her as I flopped on the couch next to Smitty. I slipped my shoe off and gave him a good head scratch with my toes while Mom set up my guitar for me next to the couch. Then Mom left to get her hair cut.

"It's a harmonica holder," said Great-grandma. "Watch this, Aven. This is called a *riff*." Then she leaned forward to put her mouth on it and started playing without even using her hands at all.

I didn't know Great-grandma could play the harmonica! "Wow, Grandma!" I exclaimed when she was done. "That was amazing! I didn't know you could play a rip!"

Great-grandma smiled. "A *riff*, honey. It's just a short melody that can be played over and over again in a song. It sounds especially good when combined with other instruments. Like say, your guitar right there."

"But how'd you learn that?" I asked.

"Your great-grandpa used to play the harmonica," she said. "He taught me a little before he passed on." Then we had a moment of silence in honor of Great-grandpa before Great-grandma said, "I wish I could play more, but all I can play is this riff."

"I think that's great!" I said. "I want to learn that riff!"

"I was hoping you'd say that," said Great-grandma. "I thought this holder would be perfect for you." Then she took the holder off herself and placed it on me.

"Um, Grandma," I said. "I think we should wash the harmonica first. There's Great-grandma spit in there."

Great-grandma nodded. "You're absolutely right, Aven." Then she pulled the harmonica off the holder, and I petted Smitty some more while she washed the spit out of the harmonica in the kitchen sink. Then she put it back in the holder, which she adjusted until it fit me.

"Now just get a feel for it first," said Great-grandma.

I tilted my head forward and blew into the harmonica. It made the coolest sounds ever! I blew and blew and blew until Great-grandma

held up a hand like she wanted me to stop. "How was that, Grandma?" I asked.

She clapped and said, "That was a wonderful start. Now, what you did was blow *into* the harmonica. If you draw in a breath instead, you'll find it makes a different sound."

I put my mouth on that harmonica again, and I blew out a big breath. Then I sucked my breath in, and Great-grandma was right! It was a totally new sound. "Cool!" I exclaimed.

Then Great-grandma showed me how the harmonica had notes in its holes. "What a coincidence, Grandma," I said. "Because the piano and guitar have letter notes, too!"

"I know," said Great-grandma, smiling. "Now, something that might be fun to do is to strum that note on the guitar, then try to match it on the harmonica. Have you learned a note yet on the guitar?"

I strummed a string and told her, "This is the E string. Luke taught me that."

Great-grandma picked up a little piece of paper from the coffee table, and I saw she had a bunch of numbers and letters on it. She said, "Let's see, that's this hole on the harmonica." Then she reached over and counted the holes on the harmonica and pointed to one. "Do you think you can blow in this hole, Aven?"

I did. "Was that E, Grandma?" I asked.

"I think so," said Great-grandma. "How about you play it and then strum the E string, and we'll see how they sound?"

But it took me a lot of tries before they both sounded like the same note. Also, it was really hard to tell if they even *were* the same note.

"That's okay," said Great-grandma. "It's not only your feet and mouth that need practice.

Your ears need practice, too. The more you practice, the more you'll learn to recognize the different notes by hearing them."

"*Phew*," I said. "Learning an instrument sure is a lot of work."

"But it can be fun work," said Great-grandma. "How about we try that riff now?"

"Can you show it to me again?" I asked.

Great-grandma raised an eyebrow and grinned. "Sure, but we'll need to wash the harmonica again because now there's Aven spit in there."

I giggled because Great-grandma was right about that. And guess what? It took the whole time I was there to learn one little riff, but I didn't give up. Even though it was really hard.

Chapter 14

Natural Musical Talent

After school the next day, Mom took me to meet a new guitar teacher. His name was Mr. Tom, and he had his own music school in the city close to the music store.

"Wow, look at that cool guitar," he said after Mom introduced us.

I looked down at the guitar I had strapped over my shoulders. "We got it in St. Louis," I said. "After we met Luke. Luke has no arms like me and plays the guitar. We went all the way to St. Louis to get barbecue sandwiches and coffee and to watch Luke play the guitar with his feet!"

"What an amazing story," said Mr. Tom.

"It is an amazing story, isn't it?" I said. "I have lots of amazing stories."

"Luke even showed her a couple of things on the guitar," said Mom.

Mr. Tom smiled. "Will you show me what you know, Aven?"

So we sat down in two chairs with the guitar at my feet, and I showed Mr. Tom how I already knew which string was the E string. "I would like to learn all the rest of the strings," I said. "But I know that might take a while."

Mr. Tom said, "I can tell you're very smart, Aven. I bet you can remember all the strings if I tell you them today."

I nodded. "I can remember because I have lots of extra brain cells."

Mr. Tom pointed at each string and told me
their letters. Then he told me all the different
parts of the guitar. "This is the *fingerboard*,"

he said. "But we can call it the toeboard for you. You see how the strings run down it, over each fret and between the nut here and the bridge here." Mr. Tom pointed out each part as he spoke.

"I'll remember all these parts," I said.

Then he showed me how when I press the strings down against the frets with my toe, it changes the *pitch* of each string. The pitch is how high or low a sound is.

Then we worked out what we should call my toes, since I don't have any fingers to name. "Finger numbering is a little different for guitar than it is for piano," said Mr. Tom. "We still use numbers, though. Except for the thumb. That one gets a letter."

"How about I give them my own names?" I said. "You know, to spice things up a bit. Make things a little more interesting."

Mr. Tom smiled. "I honestly don't see why not. What did you have in mind?"

I wiggled my big toe. "This big one is definitely Toe-mas. In your honor."

"I am definitely honored," said Mr. Tom.

Then I wiggled my second toe. "And this one I'm calling Toe-toe. Like the dog in The Wizard of Oz."

"I like it," said Mr. Tom.

Then I wiggled my middle toe. "And this tall one is called Toe-bee." I wiggled my toe next to my pinky. "And this one is Toe-jam. Because I can tell it's really going to jam on that guitar. And finally for the last one, my pinky toe."

"Let me guess," said Mr. Tom. "Toe-ry?"

I shook my head. "Nope."

"Toe-lulah?" asked Mr. Tom.

I shook my head again.

"Ot-toe?" asked Mr. Tom.

"No," I said. "This one is called Herman. Because Herman is the loveliest name in the whole wide world."

Mr. Tom pointed at each toe and repeated the names until he remembered them all. He was good at remembering, too. "You were right, Aven," he said. "This will make learning more interesting. What a good idea."

"It's like I always knew," I said. "I have natural musical talent."

Chapter 15

A Real Friend

The following week at school, I felt really super nervous. Mom and Dad just kept telling me to do my best. But what if my friends didn't think my best was good? What if they thought it was just "bad noises?" Everyone was talking about their talent, but I was quiet. Some people have called me a chatterbox, so it felt weird to keep quiet.

At recess the day before the talent show, I sat on my special swing the school bought for me. It had a back so I wouldn't have to

worry about falling off backward and crack-
ing my brain wide open. I rocked gently
back and forth, dragging my tie-dyed flats
through the sand until they started turning
a little brown.

Suddenly Emily sat down on the swing
next to me. "What's wrong, Aven?" she
asked. "Don't you want to play charades with
us? Kayla just pretended to be a wolverine,
and no one could get it 'cause no one even
knows what a wolverine acts like."

I shrugged. "I just feel like being alone," I
said.

"Are you mad at us?" she asked.

I shrugged again. "No, not really," I said.
Then I looked at her, and she looked like she
was really worried about me. I thought maybe
it was best to tell the truth. "Well, actually
you hurt my feelings."

Emily looked shocked. "Me? I hurt your feelings?"

I nodded. "When you called my piano playing bad noises," I said. "That hurt my feelings."

"I'm sorry," she said. "I was just saying what I thought."

"Maybe you don't have to say everything you think," I said. "My parents tell me sometimes I can keep those thoughts stuffed in my head when they might hurt someone's feelings, like when I didn't like the raisin clafouti."

Emily looked stumped. "But what should I have said then?" she asked.

I thought a long moment about this. "You could've said you liked my keyboard. You could've said you thought it was cool that I

can hit the keys with my toes. You could've said you could tell I was trying my best."

Emily nodded. "Next time I'll think of something better to say."

"Thank you," I said. "And even if I think your poems are terrible, even if they're the worst poems I've ever heard in my whole life, I'll think of something good to say about them."

She smiled and said, "Deal." And I felt so much better, because we should be able to tell our friends when they've hurt our feelings. And they should be able to listen. That's how I knew Emily was a real friend.

Chapter 16

Just My Best

The day of the talent show finally arrived. Robert surprised us all by *not* doing the noodle trick (I knew he was bluffing all along with that one). Instead he showed us how he can cough up a loogie and then make it drip out of his mouth super-long before sucking it right back up. Lots of people had to close their eyes while he did it, and Ms. Luna cried out, "Please don't let that drop on the carpet!"

Then Ren showed off his beautiful LEGO birds. He had a scarlet macaw, a cockatiel, and a flamingo. Then Kayla did a very cool ballet dance, and Emily read her newest poem, which she called "The Saddest Things You Ever Heard." It was about when her dog had to wear a cone on his head for a full week after he had surgery on his ear, and he got so sad that he wouldn't even play fetch or anything. I didn't actually cry, but I did have sad eyebrows the whole time she read it.

I was extra-excited when Sujata got up and sang "Somewhere Over the Rainbow."

Her voice was as beautiful as the most beautiful accordion you ever heard! And I thought maybe once I learned to play my instruments even better, she could sing some songs while I played them.

I sat in my seat, bobbing my feet and smiling at all my classmates (except for Emily, who got the sad eyebrows) so they would know that I thought their talents were awesome. I even gave Robert the best smile I could make, even though I also kind of felt like barfing.

When it was my turn, Ms. Luna helped me put on my harmonica holder and placed my new guitar at my feet in front of the class. My heart was beating so hard as I sat in my chair and started talking. "I only just started learning the guitar," I told my class. "So that means I'm not an expert yet, but I can already do this."

I strummed one of the strings with my toes and told them, "This is the E string, which is the first string. I wrote a song to go with the E string so I could remember it." I cleared my throat, and while I strummed the E string I sang, "E is the first string on the guitar. E is also the first letter in 'eat gummy bears and mint chocolate chip ice cream,' which is my first favorite thing to do." I also played E on the harmonica.

I strummed another string. "This is the B string, which is the second string. Here's the song I wrote to go with that one." I contin-ued singing while strumming the B string. "B is the second string on the guitar. B is also the second letter in 'I bet I can learn to play the guitar.'" Then I played B on the harmonica and kept strumming. I'd also made up an extra verse while watching the talent show to help me remember B. "B is also the second letter in 'I barfed when Robert hocked his loogie.'" My friends all seemed really impressed with my songwriting skills.

"There are four more strings," I said. "But I'm still working on songs for those." I cleared my throat and took a deep breath. "I still have a lot to learn about playing the guitar. I'm going to practice a lot more and keep doing my best. And in thirty-seven years, I think I'll be pretty good."

Ms. Luna laughed. "Oh, Aven," she said. "I'm so glad you're willing to put in the time and practice to learn the guitar, but I don't think it will take you quite that long to learn how to play well. As a matter of fact, I bet you'll learn a lot more before the school year is even over. Will you come back and play for us and show us all you've learned at the end of the school year?"

I nodded excitedly. "Oh yeah!" I said. "I'd love to. Also, my great-grandma bought me this cool harmonica holder and taught me about the different holes on the harmonica. She showed me how it makes different sounds if you blow out or suck in breath. One day I might even be able to play the harmonica and the guitar at the same time. She also taught me this cool riff."

Then I played the riff for the class, but I made a few mistakes. That was okay because I still had a lot to learn. My friends seemed to think it was okay, too, because they all clapped for me.

I wasn't an expert yet at playing the guitar or the harmonica, and on the day of the talent show, my performance wasn't perfect or professional. I didn't even get any money in a fishbowl. It was just my best, because my best was all I could do. And I felt pretty good about that.

Chapter 17

Just Like Mine

When we were back in our seats after lunch, I noticed that Ms. Luna was now wearing a big bulky coat, even though it wasn't very cold outside. A man I'd never seen before was with her, and he was also wearing a big coat.

Ms. Luna told us, "Class, I'd like to introduce you to Mr. Torres. Remember? I told you about Mr. Torres."

"He's your boyfriend!" Kayla called out, and the whole class started giggling. Mr. Torres giggled too.

"Nice to meet you all," said Mr. Torres. "I've heard so much about you."

"Did you put out any fires today?" someone called out.

"Did you rescue a cat?" someone else cried.

"Did you rescue a human?" another person yelled.

"Has your butt ever caught on fire?" Robert asked, and we all giggled again.

Ms. Luna gave Robert a *look*, but she was still laughing. She said to Mr. Torres, "You can see they're all very impressed that you're a firefighter."

Mr. Torres smiled and said, "And I heard they've done many impressive things today."

"Yes, they have," said Ms. Luna. Then she turned to us. "You've all inspired me with your wonderful talents today. So much so that I called Mr. Torres and asked him to come down here so we can show you *our* talents."

I was positively bursting with excitement at what they might be about to show us. "Does it have something to do with your big coats?" I asked.

"Yes, Aven," said Ms. Luna. Then she turned on a song, and she and Mr. Torres pulled their coats off. The whole class made a big *ooooohhhhh* sound because under those big coats, Ms. Luna had on the most beautiful, colorful skirt I'd ever seen in my whole entire life. And Mr. Torres had on a black suit with silver buttons.

"Oh, I know what's coming!" I cried. "Zapateado!"

Ms. Luna began tapping her feet while twirling and flinging her skirt all over the place. It was a rainbow of swirls! And Mr. Torres held his arms behind his back and moved his feet so fast that we all had to jump up to try to get a good look at them.

Mr. Torres's feet were *very* talented. Just like mine.

Chapter 18

Soccer Machine

That night at dinner, I couldn't stop talking even long enough to take a bite of pantry surprise. Tonight it looked like macaroni and cheese with canned chicken and peas mixed in. Delicious!

"And then everyone clapped, even though I wasn't the best guitar player they'd ever heard," I told my parents. "But the very best part was when Ms. Luna and her *boyfriend*," I had to pause a moment to let that thought set into my parents' heads, "danced together. It was amazing!"

"Sounds like a very exciting day," said Mom. "And we're so proud of you for showing off what you've learned on the guitar, even though you can't yet play a whole song."

"I feel proud of myself," I said. "I did my best. And guess what."

"What?" asked Dad.

"My best was good enough, after all," I said.

Mom reached over and rubbed my red head. "Of course, it was," she said.

"And to keep doing my best, I'm going to practice a lot," I said. "Because Ms. Luna said I could come back and show them what I've learned at the end of the year, and I still think maybe I can knock their socks off if I practice every day."

"You've certainly knocked my socks off," said Mom.

"You're going to have a very busy schedule starting next week, Sheebs," said Dad.

"I know!" I cried. "Guitar lessons with Mr. Tom, guitar practice every day, homework, and most exciting of all . . ."

"Soccer is starting!" Dad and I both said together.

"Watch out, world!" I said. "Here comes Aven Green Soccer Machine!"

Aven's Music Words

lyrics: the words in a song

zapateado: a Latin American style of dance that includes shoe tapping

pianist: a person who plays the piano

musical note: a single musical sound or the symbol that represents the sound

melody: a sequence of notes that sound pleasing and not like bad noises

chord: a group of notes played together

fret: the space between the metal strips on the fingerboard of a guitar

riff: a short repeated melody

fingerboard: a thin, long strip (usually made of wood) on the guitar that has strings running over it

pitch: how high or low a note is

Aven Green
can do just
about anything!

She solves
some really tricky
mysteries in

SLEUTHING MACHINE

She is an
expert baker in

BAKING MACHINE

She is a professional musican in

MUSIC MACHINE

Dusti Bowling

grew up in Scottsdale, Arizona, where, as her family will tell you, she always had her nose in a book. Dusti holds a Bachelor of Psychology and a Master of Education, but she eventually realized her true passion was writing. She is the author of *Insignificant Events in the Life of a Cactus* and *24 Hours in Nowhere*. She lives in Arizona with her husband, three daughters, a dozen tarantulas, too many scorpions, a gopher snake named Burrito, and a cockatiel named Cilantro.